Look out for other books in this series:

Charlie
& The Cat Flap

Charlie
& The Great Escape

Charlie
& The Big Snow

Charlie
& The Rocket Boy

Charlie
& The Cheese & Onion
Crisps

Charlie
& The Haunted Tent

www.hilarymckay.co.uk

Hello Charlie

Hilary McKay

Illustrated by Sam Hearn

■ SCHOLASTIC

First published in the UK in 2009
by Scholastic Children's Books
An imprint of Scholastic Ltd
Euston House, 24 Eversholt Street
London, NW1 1DB, UK
Registered office: Westfield Road, Southam, Warwickshire, CV47 0RA
SCHOLASTIC and associated logos are trademarks and/or registered
trademarks of Scholastic Inc.

Beetle and the Bear
First published by Scholastic Ltd, 2002
Text copyright © Hilary McKay, 2002

Beetle and the Big Tree
First published by Scholastic Ltd, 2002
Text copyright © Hilary McKay, 2002

Beetle and Lulu
First published by Scholastic Ltd, 2002
Text copyright © Hilary McKay, 2002

Beetle and the Hamster
First published by Scholastic Ltd, 2002
Text copyright © Hilary McKay, 2002

Text copyright © Hilary McKay, 2009
Illustrations copyright © Sam Hearn, 2009

The right of Hilary McKay and Sam Hearn to be identified as the author
and illustrator of this work has been asserted by them.

Cover illustration © Sam Hearn, 2009

ISBN 10: 1-407110-20-9
ISBN 13: 978-1-407110-20-2

Reprinted by Scholastic India Pvt. Ltd., June 2009

This is a work of fiction. Names, characters, places, incidents and dialogues
are products of the author's imagination or are used fictitiously. Any resemblance
to actual people, living or dead, events or locales is entirely coincidental.

www.scholastic.co.uk/zone

Printed at Baba Barkha Nath Printers, Bahadurgarh, Haryana.

ONE

Charlie was five years old. People said that he was not a very grown-up five. He did not act grown-up in any way.

Charlie made up songs and sang them too loud in quiet places. He ate things that should not be eaten, like paper and the sleeves of his clothes. He was useless at football. He had an old brown bear called

Bear that he carted around with him everywhere he went.

Something awful was going to happen to Charlie. He was going to start school.

All summer people had been telling Charlie that soon he would be starting school. His big brother Max had mentioned it nearly every day. His friend Henry had talked about it for weeks.

Charlie tried not to listen. He did not like the idea of school. He hoped that if he took no notice the whole daft school idea would go away.

It didn't. The last week of the summer holidays came, and then the last day. The next morning would be the first day of school.

Charlie and Max were upstairs in their bedroom.

Max was sorting out his football kit. Charlie was lying on the floor with his face buried in the stomach of his old brown bear. He was humming a terrible made-up song. It had no words and it had no tune. It was just a loud noise.

"I wish you would shut up," said Max.

Charlie hummed louder than ever, deep and noisy in the middle of his bear.

Max leaned over and dropped his football boots on Charlie's head.

Charlie added some moans to his song. It became a moaning song. It sounded awful.

Max undid his sports bottle and trickled water down the neck of Charlie's T-shirt.

Charlie stopped singing and grabbed

Max by the ankle and dragged him over.
Then he beat him round the head with
his bear. This made Max laugh. He
often laughed when Charlie attacked
him, because Charlie's attacking was so
rubbish.

Max was nine, going on ten. He was
tall and grown-up and captain of the

Junior Football Team. He had a best friend called Mike who was in the football team too. Max worried a lot about Charlie. He did not know how Charlie would manage school.

"It's going to be a lot different from playschool," he told him.

"I know."

"You won't be able to sing your awful songs."

"I know."

"Or eat your clothes."

"I know."

"Or take your bear."

"I'm taking my bear," said Charlie.

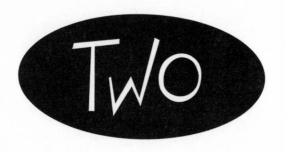

Charlie's bear was as old as Charlie. He had worn out brown fur and a chewed up nose and a brand new red and white football jumper. Charlie pushed him in and out of his school bag to see if he would fit.

"Charlie," said Max. "You'll get really laughed at! Don't take him. What if Henry sees?"

Charlie would not listen.

Morning came. Max took his football kit. Henry took his *Dr Who* pencil tin. Charlie took his bear. Luckily Henry didn't notice. He was much too excited to notice anything like that. Unlike Charlie, Henry had looked forward to this day for weeks. On the way to school Henry did not walk. Henry ran.

"What's the hurry?" demanded Charlie, puffing to keep up.

"I don't want to miss anything!" said Henry.

"Mad!" said Charlie. "Mad. Nutty. Loony. Pathetic."

Henry took no notice and rushed into the playground as if he was going somewhere wonderful.

"Bonkers," said Charlie.

At school, Mrs Price, the Class One
teacher, sat everyone down in pairs. She
sat Charlie with Henry.

"Two of a kind!" she said.

Mrs Price was wrong about that.

Out of school Charlie and Henry were

very alike. They both loved pizza and wouldn't eat yoghurt. They both sank in swimming pools even with armbands. They both could drive cars much better than their mothers, and they both had mothers who would not give them a go. They both planned to be stuntmen when they grew up. They were very alike.

But at school Henry and Charlie were opposites.

Every morning Charlie crawled to school as slowly as possible while Henry rushed so fast that the lollipop man had to slow him down with his lollipop. Every night Henry could not wait to get home and begin his homework. He read two reading books a day. Charlie did not read any books at all. He lost them. At first he lost them at home, under the cat basket, or behind the sofa. Then Max got so good at finding them that Charlie started losing them at school instead.

But Henry was as bad as Max.

"Why are you poking your book behind the radiator?" he asked nosily. "Miss, Miss, did you tell Charlie to poke... OW! Miss, Miss, Charlie pushed me!"

Henry was always calling, "Miss, Miss!" about something. It was usually something about Charlie which Mrs Price hadn't noticed. Mrs Price didn't notice a lot. She didn't notice when Charlie sat at storytime with his fingers in his ears, or when he chewed his sleeves, or when he sang his songs. She didn't even see when Charlie slid under the table and crawled across the floor and out of the door. He always headed for the cloakroom where his school bag hung. It made him feel better to open it up, and peer down for a moment at Bear's kind brown face.

He was very good at doing this invisibly. Mrs Price used to pop her head round the cloakroom door and not see a thing.

For the first few days of school Charlie managed to keep Bear a secret.

THREE

One night Max said to Charlie, "Whenever I see you at breaktime you're walking about on your own. Haven't you anyone to play with?"

"No," said Charlie. "I don't like any of them and none of them like me!"

"What about Henry?"

"Henry's the worst of all. Henry is

teacher's pet. Max?"

"Mmm?"

"Couldn't I play with you at break?"

"But I play football with Mike and the rest of the team," said Max.

"Why can't I be on the team?" asked Charlie. "You are team captain! You could make the others let me."

"Charlie," said Max patiently. "You know that you can't even kick the ball! You need more practice first. Practise with Henry."

"I don't want to practise with Henry," said Charlie. "I'm fed up of Henry. He bounces around talking all the time and asks stupid questions. And he sticks his nose in everything!"

That was true.

*

"Why is your school bag always stuffed so full?" asked Henry. "What's it got inside? Why do you keep sliding under the table? What are you chewing? Is it my rubber? Why have you got that elastic band?"

Charlie pulled back his elastic band and took aim at Henry's *Dr Who* pencil tin as if he was going to ping Dr Who on the nose.

"Don't you like Dr Who?" asked Henry. "Don't you think that's a bit weird, not liking Dr Who? Do you still have that smelly old bear that you used to bring to playschool?"

"Mind your own business!" growled Charlie, and he didn't ping Dr Who. He pinged Henry's arm instead.

"Miss, Miss!" cried Henry. "Charlie pinged my elbow with his elastic band!"

"Charlie, is that true?"

Charlie just shrugged and stared out of the window.

"I think it's nearly bleeding," said Henry, trying to lick it. "Is it red?"

"It is pinkish grey," said Mrs Price. "Go to the cloakroom and put some cold water on it. Charlie, please pass me that elastic band!"

Henry went to the cloakroom and the first thing he saw was Charlie's school bag, bulging and unguarded, hanging from its peg.

"Ha!" said Henry, and forgot all about his pinged elbow.

When he came back he was very bouncy indeed. He whispered, "Hey, Charlie! Guess what I just saw in the cloak—"

"HENRY!" said Mrs Price in such an awful voice that Henry shut up for the rest of the afternoon.

At the end of school, Charlie had to stay behind and listen to a story about Dangerous Elastic Bands. He was very worried. All the time he was listening he could hear screams of laughter coming from the playground. He rushed outside as soon as Mrs Price would let him, but it was no use. He was too late.

First he saw his school bag, flat and empty on a bench.

Next he saw Henry.

Henry was in the middle of the playground, swinging Bear round and round his head.

"Charlie's brought his teddy bear!" sang Henry, bouncing up and down.

"OY!" bellowed Charlie.

"Charlie's got a teddy!" sang Henry, and he threw Bear to Kirsty, a noisy little girl with red pigtails.

Before Charlie could reach her, Kirsty had thrown Bear to somebody else. Then Henry got him again and spun around in front of Charlie, wearing Bear like a hat.

"Charlie's brought his teddy!" sang Henry.

"Throw him to me! To me! To me!"
cried the rest of Class One, and Bear went
sailing up again.

"CHARLIE'S BROUGHT HIS TEDDY
BEAR!" they sang. "CHARLIE'S GOT A
TEDDY!"

All of a sudden Max came running out
of school, with Mike behind him.

Max saw Charlie chasing round the playground, bellowing with rage, and poor old Bear in his red and white jumper flying through the air.

For one moment Max paused, thinking, and then he knew what to do.

He charged into the middle of the group around Henry yelling, "WHAT ARE YOU KIDS DOING WITH OUR TEAM MASCOT?"

four

There was a stunned silence in the playground. Charlie stared at his brother. Henry's mouth fell open with shock. Max's friend Mike retrieved Bear and handed him to Charlie.

"Our only team mascot!" said Max loudly to Mike. "And the big match on Saturday!"

"Can you believe it?" asked Mike.

"We thought he was just Charlie's old bear," said Henry. "He *is* just Charlie's old bear!"

"That was Before," said Max.

"Before what?"

"Before now," said Max, rolling his eyes. "*Now* he is the Junior Team Mascot *wearing* the Junior Team Colours *in school* for the Junior Team Practice."

"Oh."

"Charlie," continued Max, "is the Junior Team Mascot Keeper! Isn't he, Mike?"

"Absolutely," said Mike.

"Chucking him about!" said Max, inspecting Bear carefully. "How could you? We haven't got a substitute mascot, you know!"

"No," agreed Mike, shaking his head. "No, we haven't."

Then Max and Mike looked solemn and Class One looked worried and nobody spoke until Henry squeaked, "You ought to have a substitute! You ought, Max! If you like I could bring my bear!"

Then there was a tremendous excited din as the rest of Class One also offered their bears as substitute mascots.

"Crikey, they've all got them!" said Mike.

"I don't know if we want a substitute

mascot," said Max, acting awkward. "Mascots are special! You can't just go out and buy one. Charlie keeps that bear in his bed every night!"

"I keep my Snowy in my bed every night!" said Henry, and then the rest of Class One started shouting about their bears that they kept in their beds every night.

So Max looked at Mike, and Mike looked at Max, and they said they would discuss it with the team.

five

That was how the bears came to be at school. Old bears, special bears, slept-with-every-night bears. All the bears whose owners hoped to be the Junior Football Team Substitute Mascot Keeper.

Max and Mike and the rest of the team inspected them all, and Henry's won.

Henry's bear, Snowy, was the best. The most squashed and the most tatty. And he too had a red and white striped football jumper which Henry's gran had stayed up 'til midnight to knit.

Max and Mike said it did not matter at all that Henry's mum had once washed Snowy with a red T-shirt and turned him very slightly pink.

School got much better for Charlie after that. He and Henry made friends again. Every day they took turns to visit their school bags and check on the Mascot and the Substitute Mascot.

And when the football team was photographed they were allowed to be in the picture. They sat side by side, right in the middle, grinning very proudly and holding their bears.

ONE

Charlie lived in a very small house with a
long, narrow garden. At the bottom of the
garden was a broken-down fence. On the
other side of the fence was an enormous
tree. It belonged to the Big House, where
no one had lived for years and years.

The first thing Charlie saw every
morning when he looked out of his window

was the tree with its giant-sized branches filling the sky. One day, he told his friend Henry, who lived just down the road, he would climb to the top.

"I'll come with you," said Henry. "How will we start?"

"By reaching the first branch," said Charlie.

That was the reason that the tree was so hard to climb. The first branch was high above their heads. Even with a stepladder Charlie and Henry could not quite reach. All through the half-term holidays they tried. It seemed impossible until one day Charlie had a brilliant idea.

"The biscuit tin!" he cried, and let go of the steps so suddenly that Henry, who was balanced on top, tumbled to the ground.

"OW!" cried Henry, crossly. "What are

you *doing*? Where are you going? Come back!"

But when Charlie came back with the biscuit tin and stood it carefully on the top of the stepladder, Henry forgot his bumps.

"It's exactly what we need!" he said.

"It's got chocolate gingers in, too!" said

Charlie, taking off the lid. "It's perfect!"

It was. The biscuit tin made an extra step. Now they were able to reach the first branch. Charlie had just got his arms around it when a voice called from the house, "Boys! Bedtime! Charlie, come on!"

Charlie dropped to the ground at once. He knew his mother only let them try to climb the tree because she thought they would never manage it. She would stop them if she saw that they had actually found a way to start.

"We'll do it tomorrow," he promised Henry.

But the next day it poured with rain, and the day after that Henry left for his holidays. By the time he came back for the new school term a terrible thing had happened.

TWO

The Big House was sold and people moved in. One day Charlie came home to find a new wooden fence across the end of the garden. The tree was on the other side.

"What a cheek!" said Charlie. "Boost me up, Henry, and then I'll pull you over."

But before they could do this Charlie's mother arrived.

"Sorry, boys," she said. "No climbing that fence!"

"But we need to get to the tree!" protested Charlie.

"I'm afraid you will have to find somewhere else to play," she told him. "I'm sorry about the tree. Never mind, we can still enjoy looking at it, just the same as before."

"Enjoy looking at it!" exploded Charlie, upstairs in his bedroom with Henry. "How can we enjoy looking at it when we're not allowed to climb it?"

"Pity you didn't think of that biscuit tin sooner," said Henry gloomily. "We might have climbed it if you had. Or if we hadn't stopped to eat the chocolate gingers... You had three..."

"What's that got to do with it?"

"Nothing. I just noticed you had three. While I was eating my one... Hey, look!"

There was someone crossing the Big House garden.

"It's that new boy who was in school today!" exclaimed Charlie.

"Oswald."

"Is that his name? Everyone I heard called him The Rich Kid. What's he doing?"

Oswald was wheeling a shiny red bike. Charlie and Henry watched him prop it carefully against the trunk of the tree and climb up until he was standing on the saddle.

"He's reaching up for that branch!" exclaimed Charlie, and a minute later he was running through garden yelling,

"Hey! You! That's
our tree!"

"It's not,"
said Oswald
calmly. "It's
mine. I'm going
to climb it."

"Henry and
me have been
going to climb
that tree for
years and years
and years!" said
Charlie, furiously.

"Why didn't you, then?" asked Oswald.

THREE

From that day on Charlie and Henry had
an enemy.

Oswald.

At first Oswald did not seem to
understand that he was an enemy. At
school he called, "Hi!" to Charlie and
Henry as if he was a perfectly normal
person.

Charlie and Henry ignored him then, but every day after school they would go to the end of garden and watch him fall off his bike as he tried to climb the tree. He never had long to work at it; always after a few minutes a voice called from the house, "Oswald! Quickly!" and he had to go indoors.

When Oswald was reaching for the first branch, Charlie and Henry did not ignore him. They tried to distract him. They asked him questions.

"Where's your mum and dad?"

"Work."

"Who's that in the house then?"

"Mrs Silver. She comes in to clean and do stuff."

"What's she doing now?"

"Probably cooking my tea."

"You'll ruin that bike."

"I've got other bikes."

Charlie and Henry did not have one bike between them.

"Why don't you go to a Rich Kids' school?" asked Henry rudely.

By now Oswald understood he was an enemy.

"Why don't you," he said slowly, "go to a Nosy Neighbour Big Wet Baby Rotten Horrible Jealous Kids' School?"

Then, turning his back, he climbed on to his bike, stood on the saddle, and leapt for the branch of the cedar tree.

This time he made it. For a moment he swung by his arms, and then he pulled himself up and suddenly he was high above their heads, laughing with triumph.

"I did it!" he called.

Charlie
found he had been
holding his breath. He let
it out with a whoosh. If they had
not been enemies he would have cheered.
He would have shouted, "Brilliant, Oz!"

But Charlie and Henry did not say
anything.

Oswald stopped laughing. He looked down at Charlie and Henry, who had not managed one friendly word between them, and he said, "You'd never have made it in a million years!"

Charlie and Henry turned away and went into the house.

four

Every day after that Oswald climbed
a little higher into the tree. If he saw
Charlie or Henry watching he would call
jeeringly, "You'd never have made it!"

By the end of the week he was almost
halfway up.

"What a climber!" said Max, Charlie's
big brother, watching from the window.

"He'll make it to the top any day!"

"It's not fair," said Charlie. "Me and Henry were going to climb that tree."

"You still can. Make friends with him. Maybe he'll help you."

"Help us!"

"It's a very big tree. You'd be much safer with someone who knows what they're doing!"

"Me and Henry know what we're doing," said Charlie, crossly.

"You two?" laughed Max. "You and Henry'd never make it in a million years!"

*

"Max said that?" asked Henry indignantly. "Those words? Just the same as the Rich Kid?"

"Yes. We'll show them both! We'll climb it tomorrow!"

"Tomorrow?"

"Very early in the morning. Straight after our dads go off to work. We'll go all the way up and stick a flag on the top."

"What sort of flag?"

"One that says 'CHARLIE AND HENRY WERE HERE!'"

"Or 'HENRY AND CHARLIE'?"

Charlie made a flag out of a pillowcase with felt-tip pen writing. On one side it said 'CHARLIE AND HENRY'. On the other it said 'HENRY AND CHARLIE'. On both sides it said 'WERE HERE!'

"OK?" he asked Henry.

"OK," said Henry.

five

It was hard sneaking out of their houses
the next morning, but still, they managed
it. They met at the bottom of Charlie's
garden, Charlie clutching the biscuit tin,
Henry carrying the flag. The stepladder,
ready from the night before, was lifted over
the fence. The boys followed afterwards,
tumbling on to the thick damp grass.

"Are you scared?" asked Henry.

"Me?" asked Charlie boastfully, balancing the biscuit tin on top of the steps and beginning to climb. "Scared of what?" and he swung himself on to the first branch as if he had been doing it all his life.

"Are you scared, then?" he asked, reaching down a hand to pull up Henry.

Henry did not reply until he was safely beside Charlie. Then he said, just as boastfully, "Scared of what?" and they both began to laugh. "Scared?" they asked each other, and set off climbing higher into the tree.

It was easier for them than it had been for Oswald. He had been climbing alone, in a hurry. They could help each other, and they did not have to rush. No one was going to shout at them; no one knew they were there.

As they went higher the branches grew closer together. It was like a giant climbing frame. Charlie felt as if he could carry on for ever.

Then suddenly, everything changed.

"There's Suzy, our cat," said Charlie.

Suzy was on the bedroom window sill. She was looking up at them. She looked very small.

"This tree is higher than your house," said Henry.

"Yes," said Charlie, and

he glanced up. They were very near the top. A little breeze had begun, and the tree was moving. Charlie felt a tingly, cold feeling all down his spine.

"Only a little way more," said Henry, but Charlie did not move. Instead he clung tightly and tried to concentrate on the cat. She stood up, stretched lazily along the narrow sill, and jumped.

That made Charlie and Henry look down, and for the first time they saw just how high they had climbed. It made their knees shake, and their hands go cold, and their heads feel strange and dizzy. Henry dropped his pillowcase flag and it floated like a feather all the way to the ground.

"I'm going to fall!" cried Charlie.

Six

In his sleep, Oswald heard
Charlie's cry. He rolled
out of bed and went
to the window.
At once he saw
Charlie and
Henry, high in
the tree, hanging
on for their lives.

Oswald completely forgot that he was their enemy, and he rushed out of the house, up the stepladder and straight on to the first branch of the cedar tree.

"Don't move!" he cried, and swung himself up, faster than he had ever climbed before.

Looking at Oswald instead of looking at the ground made Charlie and Henry feel better. Their dizziness began to fade.

"Nearly there!" called Oswald, and just as he said it, he slipped.

"*Hold on,*" shouted Charlie, but Oswald could not stop. He slid bouncing from branch to branch, faster and faster.

The branches shook as he hit them.

Henry shut his eyes because he could not bear to look.

Charlie saw Oswald reach for the

lowest branch, lose his grip and fall. Then came a sound like a horrible crunch, and there was Oswald, spread out like a starfish on the grass below.

"Oz!" shouted Charlie, and hurried down the tree almost as fast as Oswald had fallen, grabbing and jumping, calling, "Oz! Oz!"

He came to the last branch, swung down his legs, and dropped to the ground. Henry followed a second later.

Oswald's eyes were shut.

"Oz!" said Charlie, while Henry mopped Oswald's head with the pillowcase flag. "Oz, are you alive ... or are you ... are you...?"

"Dead?" asked Henry, fearfully.

"Not dead," said Oswald, and opened his eyes.

Henry sighed with relief, but Charlie was still frightened.

"Oz," he said. "There was an awful crunch when you landed. I think you must have broken something. You'd better lie still."

Oswald did not lie still. He sat up and pulled something out from underneath him.

It was the biscuit tin, squashed flat.

Then he lay down again and began to shake with laughter.

Charlie and Henry joined in. They laughed because they were safe, and because they were not enemies, and because the biscuit tin was broken, but Oz was safe. They laughed until it hurt.

Then they ate up all the biscuits, even the ones that were squashed to crumbs, and they made friends, there on the grass, under the tree.

*

"Oz," said Charlie, "have you really got more than one bike?"

"I've got three," said Oz.

He did not say it like a Rich Kid. He just said it like a boy with a lot of bikes.

"We can ride one each," said Oz.

.

ONE

Charlie was having a terrible time. He
was having his hair cut.

"As short as possible," his mother told
the hairdresser, "because goodness knows
when I will get him here again."

There were tickly bits in Charlie's eyes.
There was a frightened tingle on one of
his ears where he had moved at the wrong

time and nearly got snipped.

"Nearly done," said the hairdresser and reached out a hand to pick something up.

"What...?" began Charlie, but he did not finish the question because suddenly there was a noise like a million wasps.

And the wasps were on Charlie's neck, and he felt hotness and weirdness and an awful buzzing fierceness.

"WAAAAHHHH!!!" shouted Charlie, and leaped from his seat.

And shot across the shop.

And out of the door.

And down the street yelling, "GET OFF! GET OFF!"

After Charlie ran his big brother Max.

And after Max ran their mother (it was the first time in her life that she had ever

run out of a shop without paying).

And in the doorway of the shop stood the hairdresser, and the other hairdresser, and the girl who swept up the chopped-off bits and the other girl who looked after the desk.

And they said to each other, "He won't be back!"

Charlie's hair grew longer and longer. It grew in tufts and lumps, past his ears and on to his shoulders. It blew in his eyes and dangled in his dinner. It looked awful.

"I like the way it looks," said Charlie.

At home his mum moaned about it.

At school people joked about it.

Sam was the biggest, toughest boy in

the class. He had bright red hair that grew in spikes. He joked about Charlie's hair most of all.

He said, "Hey, Charlie, you look just like one of the girls."

And he lifted chunks of Charlie's hair, and asked, "Anyone in under there?"

And one day he found a pink sparkly hairclip in the playground, and later that afternoon when the classroom was full of slanting sunshine, and everyone was hot and half asleep, he wandered past Charlie and clipped the pink sparkly clip into the the middle of his hair.

Charlie's new hair decoration was not noticed at first. Not until Sam called across the room, "Oh, Charlie, that looks cool!"

Then everyone noticed.

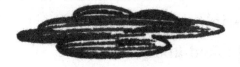

And everyone laughed.

Even the teacher.

So Charlie yanked the clip out of his hair and threw it hard across the room.

And then Charlie was in trouble.

All because of his hair.

"If I were you," advised his friend Henry after school that day, "I'd give in and get it cut."

But Charlie was not a giving in sort of person, and the more people tried to make him, the more he wouldn't.

"It's my hair and I like it like this and you can't make me," said Charlie.

Charlie's mother bought a Do-It-Yourself haircutting kit from Boots.

It vanished.

Charlie's brother Max chopped off a chunk while Charlie was asleep.

Charlie chopped off a chunk from Max while he was asleep.

A big chunk.

That stopped Max messing about with Charlie's hair.

At school Sam said:

"Tie it in a ponytail."

"Knit it into a hat!"

"Feed it to a donkey!"

"Dangle it from the window and see who climbs up!"

"Get it cut," advised Henry.

"He can't," said Sam very rudely. "Don't you know, hairdressers won't cut HAIR WITH NITS!"

THREE

Charlie was very interested to hear that
hairdressers wouldn't cut hair with nits.
He was tired of being told what to do with
his own, home-grown hair. He thought
nits might solve all his problems.

He would go to the hairdressers' (he
imagined).

With his secret nit supply.

And the hairdresser would take one look and say, "Take him away! I refuse to cut that hair!"

And then everyone would have to leave him alone.

"How do you get nits?" he asked Henry, who often had them.

"Oh," said Henry. "It's easy. They just arrive. Like weather."

"Then what happens?"

"I don't know. My mum always does a nit attack and zaps them."

"Next time you have some will you share them with me?"

"OK," said Henry cheerfully, "but your mum will hate them."

"I'll keep them secret."

"It's very, very hard to keep them secret," said Henry.

And that was true.

Henry got nits.

And shared them with Charlie.

And Charlie's nits walked about all over his head with their itchy feet. They explored behind his ears and they made camps on the top of his head. They walked all day and they walked all night, and they were impossible to keep secret.

AAARRGH

"Told you so!" said Henry.

Charlie's mother and Henry's mother had a nit-zapping afternoon in

Charlie's garden.

Charlie and Henry's heads were scrubbed with terrible nit shampoo and combed with terrible combs. Charlie's head took ten times longer than Henry's to comb, because he had ten times more hair. This made Charlie's mother mad.

"Fancy!" she snapped. "A great big boy like you, scared to go to the hairdressers'!"

"Is he scared?" asked Henry, very surprised. "I thought he liked it like that!"

"I do!" growled Charlie. "And I am NOT scared. Don't you go round school telling people I'm scared! 'Specially not Sam!"

"Why 'specially not Sam?" asked Henry.

"Just because."

"I shan't tell Sam anything," said Henry, but the very next day he did.

four

Charlie and Henry quarrelled at school the next day, but it was not their fault.

It was the spider's fault.

The spider was walking down a corridor where Charlie couldn't help seeing it. And once Charlie had seen it, he could not resist picking it up. And once he had picked it up, the best thing to do

with it, Charlie thought, was to pop it into
Henry's sandwich box, for a lunchtime
surprise. Even though he knew quite well
that spiders were not Henry's favourite
animals.

Henry made a most enormous fuss
about the spider in his lunch box.

"What a lot of bother about one tiny
little spider!" said Charlie.

"You can shut up!" yelled Henry (right in front of Sam). "You are ten million times more scared of hairdressers than I am of spiders!"

"Is he?" asked Sam.

"Yes, he is!" said Henry.

"No, I'm not!" said Charlie.

"Is that why he won't get his hair cut?" asked Sam.

"No, it isn't," said Charlie. "It's my hair and I like it like this. I'll get it cut when I want."

"Do it then," said Sam.

"Dare you!" said Henry.

"Double dare," said Sam.

When Sam said, "Double dare", Charlie knew he had to.

He didn't want to. He hated the idea. He was scared. But all the same, he asked his mum, "When can I get my hair cut?"

"The sooner the better," said Charlie's mum. "Saturday. First thing."

"Saturday, first thing," Charlie told Sam at school.

"Saturday," said Sam. "I'm coming to watch."

"You can't! You can't just go to a hairdressers' to watch!"

"I can if I have mine cut too," said Sam.

five

Saturday morning was bright and hot.

It was a perfect day for deep-sea diving
in the paddling pool with straws for
snorkels, which was something Charlie
had been wanting to try for ages.

It was a perfect day for getting as many
people as possible together in the street for a
massive water fight, which was Max's idea.

It was a perfect day, said Henry',
coming round to call for Charlie, for
building a jungle camp. Or climbing on to
the shed roof and signalling to aeroplanes.
Or treasure hunting with his metal
detector which had new batteries at last.

"I can't do any of those things," said
Charlie crossly. "Because YOU dared me
and Sam double
dared me to go and
get my hair cut.
What a waste of a
perfect day!"

"I'm surprised
you can even
tell that the sun
is out, under
all that heap
of hair!" said

Charlie's mum. "It's a perfect day to get it cut! And you can do all those other things afterwards."

That did not cheer up Charlie. He was too worried about Now to think about Afterwards. He sulked all the way to the hairdressers, thinking about being combed.

And chopped.

And buzzed up the back.

And all with Sam watching.

Sam already waiting at the hairdressers'
when Charlie slid in behind his mother.

"Never thought I'd see you again!" said
the hairdresser, recognizing Charlie at once,
and he asked his mum, "How much off?"

"The more the better," said Charlie's
mum. "But you'd better ask Charlie. This
is all his idea."

Sam's mum said the same when Sam's hairdresser asked how much he should cut.

"Ask Sam," she said. "He dragged me here."

Then Charlie's mum and Sam's mum escaped to the waiting place to read magazines and chat and get away from Charlie and Sam.

Charlie and Sam did not say a word to each other, but Sam grinned as he climbed into his chair.

Charlie didn't grin. Charlie shivered. He felt like running away, but he couldn't because there was Sam, right beside him, and Sam's reflection, watching from the mirror.

Sam-in-the-mirror made chopping signs with his fingers at Charlie's head. Charlie-in-the-mirror glared back.

Charlie's hairdresser asked, "Are you two friends?"

"NO!" said Charlie.

Sam's hairdresser asked, "What's going on, then?"

"It's a dare," said Sam.

"A double dare," said Charlie.

"A double dare!" repeated the two hairdressers, and they looked at each other and laughed.

Then the terrible cutting began.

The two hairdressers kept up with each other. Sam's cut slowly, because Sam had not much hair to start with. Charlie's cut fast, because Charlie had such heaps. Sam kept his eyes open, watching, but Charlie screwed his tight shut. It was the only way he could bear it.

But even with his eyes shut he could not help hearing.

The radio singing songs to itself.

The mothers chattering.

The slow snip, snip of the scissors round Sam's head.

The fast, crunching, munching sound of the blades round his own.

"You can look now!" said his hairdresser at last. "You're just about done."

So Charlie opened his eyes and the

81

first thing he saw was Sam-in-the-mirror grinning and making chopping signs at Charlie's head.

Then Charlie stopped being frightened of hairdressers suddenly and for ever, and he became very fierce instead.

He looked at Sam's reflected head, and he looked at his own, and he said, "I'd like my hair even shorter, please."

So Sam looked at Charlie and said, "Even shorter, please", too.

And he stopped smiling.

More hair came off Charlie's head.

More hair came off Sam's.

Now the mirrors were full of glaring eyes.

"Shorter still, if you don't mind," said Charlie, when the scissors stopped once more.

"Much, much shorter," said Sam, a minute or two later.

Hair fell from Charlie and Sam like itchy rain. Around Sam's chair was a circle of bright red spikes. Around Charlie's was a haystack of blackness. In the mirror Sam's face grew more and more thoughtful. In the mirror Charlie made chopping signs at Sam's head.

Then Sam's hairdresser put his scissors down, and Sam gave a great sigh like he had been holding his breath. He didn't look thoughtful now. He looked worried. He didn't want any more hair cut off, Charlie could tell.

So Charlie said to his hairdresser, "Please could you buzz me at the back with a razor?"

And Sam said, "You win!"

And, to Charlie's utter astonishment,
he climbed down from his chair and stood
and watched in admiration while Charlie
had all his hair buzzed off
at the back with a razor.

"I just don't like that
buzzer," Sam said.

Suddenly,
Charlie liked
Sam very
much indeed.
And he was
sorry for him
too.

"Get yours
buzzed as well!" he told him. "Go on! It's
not that bad! It doesn't hurt! It's only like
a million wasps landing on your neck!
Dare you! Dare you! Double dare!"

So in the end, Sam did.

And then they went and frightened their mothers.

And after that they went home together.

Where both of them kindly helped Henry cut his hair.

And after that they did treasure hunting, and aeroplane signalling, and built a camp and went snorkelling. And they had an enormous water fight with everyone in the street.

And it was a perfect day.

ONE

In Charlie's house there were four people. Charlie, his big brother Max, and his mum and dad.

There was also one pet, Suzy the cat.

Once there had been two pets. Once, long ago, there had been a hamster.

The hamster lived in a cage on top of the fridge, safe from Suzy.

Until Suzy learnt to jump on fridges.

And to open hamster-cage doors.

Suzy learnt this all in one night. (She
was a very clever cat.)

Suzy was not at all hungry for breakfast
the next morning.

And although Charlie and Max hunted
inside and out, upstairs and down, for
weeks and weeks and weeks, not a whisker
of that hamster was ever seen again.

So in the end the carpets were fixed
back down to the floor, and the washing
machine was screwed together again
and the heaps of books were put back in
the bookcases. And all the other things
that Charlie and Max had pulled out,
or emptied, or taken to pieces were put
back together again. And a gravestone in

memory of Hammy was built out of Lego and planted in the garden.

And people stopped crying and getting up in the night to see if something awful was happening.

And Charlie's mother said, "Suzy did not mean to make you so sad. She was only being a cat. And from now on this is the Law on Pets:

> *One is Enough*
> *And THAT is THAT*
> *Any More than One is MUCH Too*
> *Stressful!"*

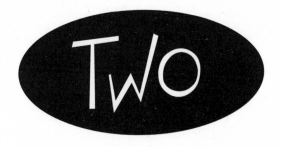

In a house close by to Charlie's lived a girl called Lulu. Charlie knew her very well. She was in his class at school, and she sometimes played out in the street. But she did not play out often because she was so busy looking after the zoo.

That was what Charlie and Henry called Lulu's house. The zoo.

Lulu's mother was the opposite of Charlie's mother when it came to the Law on Pets.

This was Lulu's mother's Law on Pets:

The More the Merrier
As Long as Lulu Cleans Them Out

Lulu was a good zookeeper. She cleaned out the zoo animals and played with them. She invented toys to stop them being bored and remembered their birthdays.

But even though Lulu worked so hard there were sometimes problems in her zoo.

The biggest problem was that it was so large. Parents said to children playing at Lulu's house, "Please don't let Lulu give you a rabbit. Or lend you a gerbil. Don't come home with that jam jar of stick insects that you brought with you last time. We don't want any more dogs for sleepovers. We don't need any more fish."

When people visited Lulu they always asked the same question, "Anything new?"

"Anything new?" asked Charlie one day, and Lulu said, "Yes! You'll never guess!

You know that big fat white rabbit that we found in a box on the doorstep? Seven babies! Just like that!"

The rabbit babies looked like snowballs with pink jelly-bean eyes.

"Now come and see the gerbils!" said Lulu. "You know I had two because they were buy one get one free? Well, look! A whole family!"

Charlie admired the gerbils, played with the dogs, and tried with Lulu to count the fish.

And then they came to the hamster.

"Oh!" exclaimed Charlie. "That's exactly like my old hamster!"

"He's a rescue hamster," said Lulu.

"A what?" asked Charlie, looking very closely.

"A rescue hamster. He came from that

pet rescue place called The Ark. They take in pets and look after them until they find them new homes. Both our dogs came from there. They were strays..."

"Strays?"

"You know, lost."

"Lost," said Charlie, and he and the hamster stared at each other, thinking.

"Lost," repeated Charlie. "I lost a hamster once. Ages ago. He was called Hammy. What this one called?"

"Toffee," said Lulu, and gave Toffee a nut tightly wrapped in paper so that he had the interesting job of unwrapping it as well as the prize of the nut. "Are you coming to look at the parrot?"

"I might just stay here," said Charlie, and settled down to watch Toffee tear open his parcel.

He really was very like Hammy indeed. Just the same hamsterish size. Just the same golden fur. Just the same teddy bear shape...

"I wonder what happened to Hammy," said Charlie.

THREE

Charlie went to look for Henry, his best friend. He found him in his house, lying on the sofa with two grazed knees, being rather grumpy.

"You know what happened to Hammy," said Henry, "we all do! The fuss you made at school! No one could talk about cats or pets for days and days!"

"Oh shut up!"

"Or ham!"

"I never made a fuss about ham!"

"Yes you did! And what about the whole class having to watch *The Lion King* that everyone had seen a million times already so as you could learn about the circle of life!"

"I'll be careful of your knees," said Charlie, and picked up a sofa cushion and hit Henry everywhere else as hard as he could.

"Suzy ate Hammy!" shouted Henry at every chance he got between whacks. "OW! Grabbed him in the dark! Get off! Chewed him up! Chomp, chomp! Swallowed like mad... Let go!"

Howling, they crashed off the sofa together.

"HENRY!" called a voice from the kitchen. "Just lying quietly, Mum!" called Henry, lying quietly on the sofa.

"What I was thinking," said Charlie, as if nothing at all had happened, "was that we don't really know that Suzy ate Hammy. No one actually saw her do it. He just disappeared."

"And Suzy didn't want any breakfast."

"Mmm."

"Anyway, that hamster of Lulu's is Toffee. Not Hammy. So."

"Yes," agreed Charlie, *but who called him Toffee?*"

"What?"

But Charlie was gone, running back to Lulu's house so fast that Henry with his sore knees did not even try to follow.

Lulu was building the gerbils a playground when Charlie rushed in.

"*Who called him Toffee?*" he demanded.

"I did," said Lulu, calmly.

"But what was he called before that?"

"Don't know," said Lulu, chopping a cereal box into a maze.

"I think," said Charlie, "I think he was called HAMMY!"

"Like your Hammy?"

"I think," said Charlie, "he *is* my Hammy! That's what I think!"

Lulu looked at Toffee in astonishment.

"I think he's my Hammy that got lost and that rescue place found and you brought here and called Toffee! I've worked it all out with Henry!"

Lulu was not only very good at getting pets, she was also fantastic at giving them away. In only a moment she had captured Toffee and handed him to

Charlie. Two black and white mice were lifted out of a biscuit tin and popped into Toffee's cage. A cabbage leaf and some caterpillars went into the biscuit tin.

"There!" said Lulu.

FOUR

The first thing Henry said was, "What about your mum's Law on Pets?"

The second thing he said was, "That's not Hammy."

Charlie said, "I'd forgotten my rubbish mum's rubbish Law on Pets", and "It's Hammy."

Henry said, "That can't be Hammy

because Suzy ate him. Anyway Hammy
didn't look like that. He was much
scruffier."

"He wasn't!" said Charlie, juggling
Hammy between his hands.

"With tatty old ears!'

"He hadn't!" said
Charlie, wriggling
as Hammy shot up
a sleeve, out of his
collar, and scrabbled
round his neck.

"Hammy kept
still," said Henry.
"He was a very quiet
hamster. That one is
much bouncier!"

"He's excited to
see me, that's why!"

"It's just not fair, you having two pets while I have none!"

"Borrow him then," said Charlie, passing him over. "While I go home and fetch his old cage. It's in our shed somewhere. I won't be long."

"Be ages!" said Henry, but Charlie found the cage quite quickly.

"And what are you planning to do with that?" asked his mother, suddenly appearing. "I hope Lulu hasn't gone and given you a hippopotamus or something, because I really couldn't stand the strain!"

"No, no," said Charlie, "I'm just taking it to Henry's, that's all," and he escaped before she could ask any more difficult questions.

"Mum's in one of her moods!" he told

Henry, as they made Hammy comfortable with sawdust and hamster food borrowed from Lulu. "I think I'd better keep him secret for a while. There you are, Ham! I bet you're glad to be back in your old cage again!"

Hammy did not act glad. He grabbed the bars and gnawed them, making a sound like a loud electric drill.

"That'll be hard to keep secret," said Henry.

"He'll go to sleep soon," said Charlie. "He sleeps an awful lot, Hammy does."

Hammy did not go to sleep. He kicked sawdust out of the cage in fountains and gnawed louder than ever.

"He's bored," said Henry. "Let's give him a run in the garden."

Charlie explained that Hammy was not

a running sort of hamster.

"He just stands around and chews things," he said, but Henry would not listen. He insisted on letting Hammy out of the cage, and once Hammy was free he did not stand around and chew anything. He raced across the grass, making for the worst place in the garden.

The worst place in the garden was the compost heap. It was made of soggy leaves and vegetable peelings, old tea bags, banana skins, black grass and slugs.

"Catch him or he'll be lost for ever!" cried Henry, and Charlie dived.

It was like diving into an enormous smelly pudding.

Hammy did not want to come out of the compost pudding. For a long time he raced up and down, and round and round, always managing to keep just in front of Charlie's grabbing hands. And for some reason the compost did not seem to stick on him. He kept perfectly clean.

Charlie did not. Then Hammy got tired of the compost heap and made a dash for the dark space under the shed.

The space under the shed was the second worst place in the garden. It was very narrow. Charlie lay down on his stomach and peered into the darkness.

"You'll have to crawl," said Henry.

"You should. You let him go!"

"I can't because of my sore knees," said Henry, so Charlie had to do it.

Under the shed was horrible. Musty and cobwebby. Dust filled Charlie's eyes and nose and crawly things ran across his bare neck.

"Hurry!" commanded Henry.

"How can I hurry, stuck under this shed?" demanded Charlie. "I can't even see! Ouch!"

"What?"

"I'm hooked on something sharp."

"Go backwards! Oh, here's Hammy, just popped out right by me... Hammy! Hammy! ... Charlie!"

"What?"

"You can come out! I've got him!'

Coming out was terrible. Backwards

was impossible, but by ripping his T-shirt away from whatever had hooked him Charlie managed to move forwards little by little.

He dragged himself into daylight at last, and just as he did so, Henry's dad's oily old bike fell down on top of him.

"OOOOWWWWWW!" moaned Charlie. "Help me, Henry!"

Henry did help. He forgot his sore knees, put the hamster in his pocket, and dragged the bike off Charlie's head. He shooed a live beetle out of his hair, and flicked away two dead spiders. He said, "That T-shirt looked awful anyway", and found the trainer that Charlie had lost. He even tried brushing away the compost and cobwebs and dirt.

"Thanks," said Charlie.

"And I've got your hamster safe," said Henry proudly, and tipped him gently into Charlie's hand.

Then Hammy (who before had been famous for never biting) bit Charlie very hard indeed.

five

"He wasn't Hammy after all," said Charlie, sadly, to Lulu. "Henry was right. He only looked like him; he didn't act like him one bit."

"Poor Charlie," said Lulu, and Suzy, who had been listening in an interested kind of way, rubbed her furry head against his bandaged hand.

"Anyway, I've given him to Henry," continued Charlie, stroking Suzy. "For a get-well present because of his knees. He was very pleased. Do you mind?"

"Not at all," said Lulu. "Would you like to come and look at the rabbit babies again?"

"I don't really want a rabbit, thanks Lulu."

"The gerbils are sweet."

"I know, but Suzy..."

"Well, what about fish! We'll dig you a pond."

"I tried to dig a pond once before," said Charlie. "It didn't work. I couldn't keep the water in. I filled it up about a million times and then I gave up."

"Stick insects, then? They just need a jam jar."

"Stick insects, make my mum go freaky," said Charlie, picking up Suzy and hugging her, "And anyway, my mum has this law about pets. She says 'One is Enough. And THAT is THAT. Any More than One is MUCH Too Stressful!'

"And I think she may be right," said Charlie.

Meet Charlie – he's trouble!

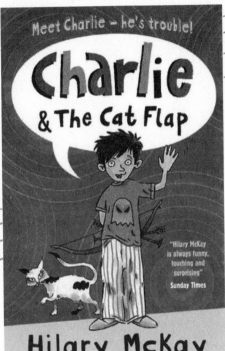

Charlie and Henry are staying the night at Charlie's house. They've made a deal, but the night doesn't go quite as Charlie plans...

Meet Charlie – he's trouble!

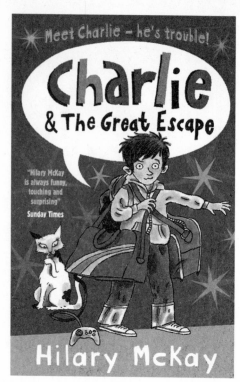

Charlie's fed up with his mean family always
picking on him – so he's decided to run away.
That'll show them! Now they'll be sorry!

But running away means being boringly,
IMPOSSIBLY quiet…

Meet Charlie – he's trouble!

Meet Charlie – he's trouble!

Charlie
& The Big Snow

Hilary McKay

"The snow's all getting wasted! What'll we do? It will never last till after school!"

Charlie's been waiting for snow his whole life, but now it's come, everyone's trying to spoil it! Luckily, Charlie has a very clever plan to keep it safe...

Meet Charlie – he's trouble!

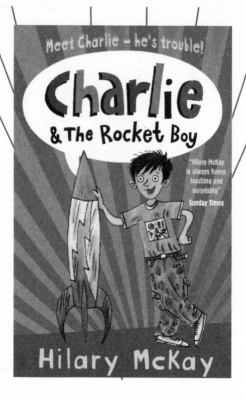

*"Zachary is a liar, liar,
pants on fire!"*

There's a new boy in Charlie's class. Zachary
says his dad is away on a rocket but Charlie
knows that's rubbish... Isn't it?

Meet Charlie – he's trouble!

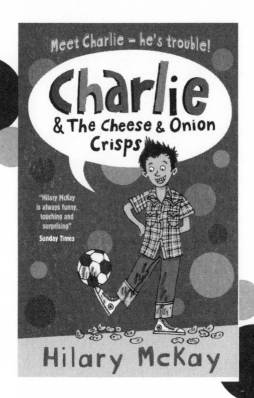

*Charlie has given up
cheese and onion crisps!*

He just hasn't been himself lately.
There's only one thing for it – the Truly
Amazing Smarties Trick!

Meet Charlie – he's trouble!

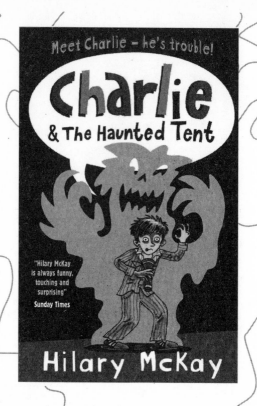

Meet Charlie – he's trouble!

Charlie
& The Haunted Tent

"Hilary McKay is always funny, touching and surprising"
Sunday Times

Hilary McKay

Charlie's big brother Max isn't scared of anything ... except Aunt Emma's spooky house.

At last it's Charlie's chance to be the hero.
Those ghosts had better watch out!